KAIJU APOCALYPSE II

ERIC S BROWN
JASON CORDOVA

KAIJU APOCALYPSE II

Around him, the world crumbled and burned, and there was nothing he could do about it.

Captain Nathan Whitmire gasped as the last bit of cryo-sleep began to wear off, his higher brain functions pushing the subconscious reactions to the back as he became aware of his surroundings and his location. His lungs burned as they took their first breath of true oxygen. His throat felt raw and abused. Strength slowly returned to his body as his nervous system came fully online. With that strength, though, came the realization that he was still alive.

Instead of opening his eyes, however, he reached for the dream that had been tormenting him. He knew that scientists believed that when the subconscious mind dominated during a long cryo-sleep, a sort of "precognitive" experience could occur when the changeover began. It was a very rare experience, but Nathan knew that it was always accurate – if the memory could be retained. Science could not explain it, and it was the rare individual who could remember the dream.

Unfortunately, the last vestiges of this particular dream slipped from his mental fingers, gone forever.

"Good morning, Captain Whitmire," a hollow, yet cheerful sounding voice greeted him as he woke up. It belonged to the *Argo's* artificial intelligence system, Medea.

His mind drifted back to the faded memory. Something bad was about to happen, he recalled. However, the rest of the dream eluded him. That memory washed out as well as his mind came fully aware of his surroundings.

Nathan stretched out his arms and struggled to wiggle his toes as the cryo-juice was flushed from his system. His stomach gurgled noisily, reminding him that, if all had gone well, it had been over seventeen months since he had last eaten. An intense pressure was suddenly applied to his bladder and a soft moan passed unbidden through his lips.

There was no way around it. The human body was not designed for cryo-sleep, and coming out of it was one of the most painful experiences outside of childbirth. His skin felt like it was on fire as every single nerve in his extremities came alive. If he could have screamed, he would have. Fortunately for his dignity, his vocal cords were not yet up to snuff for any sort of screaming. The pain slowly became manageable as the moments passed, and finally went away fully. He cracked open his eyes and slowly went through his mental checklist.

"Relax, Captain," Medea tried to soothe him as his fingers began to twitch and respond to his commands. "The cryo-juice is almost completely out of your system. In eight seconds, you should have full control over your motor skills once more. How are you feeling?"

Nathan didn't answer, focusing instead on his left big toe. It was a trick he had learned when he had come out of cryo for the very first time during the trial runs. If he could focus on something small and typically ignored, the rest of the pain would drift away.

"How long has it been, Medea?" Nathan asked as the last wave of pain went away. His tongue felt thick and his jaw was sore, but that was to be expected. He had not used it in a very long time.

"You have been in cryo-sleep for one year, five months, two days–"

"Thanks," Nathan said, cutting the AI off. "That's good enough. Give me a SITREP, starting with structural integrity of the *Argo*."

"Structural integrity of the hull is at satisfactory levels," Medea began, her voice still cheerful as Nathan swung his legs over the edge of his bed and stood up. The room spun slightly as blood rushed to his head. He grabbed one of the overhead handles and waited for the sudden bout of dizziness to pass. Meanwhile, Medea continued to drone on. "Environmental levels in occupied sections are nominal. Oxygen levels are coming up to hospitable levels at primary duty stations throughout the *Argo*. Engineering is showing green on all four engines, and both the primary and secondary bridges are fully powered. All stations, save one, report green beds. There was one catastrophic failure of a cryo-sleep bed, Portside Section, Subsection D, resulting in a singular fatality due to irreparable damage to the vagus nerve, and thus causing a complete nervous system failure. Resuscitation was not possible. Notification of the death has been passed on to the Medical Board."

"Damn," Nathan grunted as he grabbed his uniform from the storage closet. He quickly pulled on his trousers and buttoned up his blouse. "Medea, who was the individual that died?"

"Engineering Apprentice Bahwoh Buhtan Woods, Captain."

Nathan shook his head. "Never heard of her."

"Him, actually, Captain," Medea corrected in a gentle tone. "Single, nineteen years of age. Family origins were from Liberia, a member of the ruling National Humanist Movement before he emigrated to Lemura Base after the fall of Abidjan. Completed his first apprenticeship just before the *Argo* left Earth, though he was not one of the engineers who were wakened upon our arrival at Alpha Centauri. He left no dependents."

"Thank God for small favors," Nathan muttered as he rubbed his scalp. "All right, let's get up to speed."

"We are currently in a heliosynchronous orbit of Earth," Medea began. "The *Argo* is currently stationed at four hundred kilometers above the Earth's surface and is maintaining a constant speed of 11,973 kilometers per hour. The *Argo* is currently above Pacifica Base, and soon shall be moving into position above Lemura Base, then crossing paths with Atlantica Base. I am currently running diagnostics on our communications system due to unknown anomalies, which are interfering with connectivity of any relay on Earth, or to any of the satellites which are still in orbit."

"Wait," Nathan paused while lacing up his boots. "Is it an issue on our end or Earth's?"

"Unknown at this time," Medea replied.

"Well, that's great," Nathan grunted and finished putting his boots on. He bloused his trousers and stood up. "Okay, run an internal diagnostics and wake up a sensor team to run a diagnostics on our own relay in case this is a hardware issue. Also, continue waking vital crew of the ship as per standard operating procedures. How long will your internal diagnostics take?"

"Five minutes, eleven seconds," Medea responded.

"Okay," Nathan nodded. "Do it. How long until the sensor team is up and about?"

"I took the liberty of waking them already, sir," Medea stated. "I was unable to initially identify any type of radio transmissions upon clearing the asteroid belt. Even accounting for the fourteen minute delay when we passed Ceres, there has been no radio waves detected in the time since."

"You're not picking up *any* radio signals or laser transmissions?" Nathan asked, surprised.

"Correct."

"Do we have any visuals of Pacifica, Atlantica or Lemura yet? Or any of the bases?"

"I have visuals of Pacifica Base stored in my memory banks, Captain," Medea answered. "Bringing them online now."

Nathan walked over to his console and watched as the image of the base appeared on screen. He frowned and zoomed in on the image. His frown deepened as he stared at the screen, his mind not comprehending what he was seeing. Pacifica was there, yet the walls appeared to be ruined. There were life forms in the streets, but they were shorter than he expected to see, bulkier somehow.

Pacifica had fallen, it appeared. Nathan's heart grew cold in his chest. If Pacifica had fallen, then the smaller bases did not stand a chance.

"How long until we pass over Lemura?" Nathan asked, his voice suddenly hoarse.

"Fourteen minutes," Medea answered. Nathan swore softly.

"Okay, let's start waking up vital personnel only," Nathan ordered. "Keep the colonists and non-essential crew in cryo for the time being. Also, wake up Governor Trion. Begin operating under Gamma Protocols until we have more information. Everything we have in the visual banks are now classified Top Secret and above."

"Yes, Captain," Medea said. "Might I remind you that the Gamma Protocols require some sort of civilian oversight of all military personnel?"

"I know that, Medea," Nathan replied. "That's why I had you wake up Governor Trion and only the governor. She'll function as my oversight, and I can control one civilian much easier than I can a dozen."

"I am not entirely certain that is why this protocol was written this way..." the AI's voice tapered off. Nathan smiled grimly.

"I'm violating the spirit of the law," Nathan told the machine, "not the letter. It's a human thing."

"Indeed." If AI's could sigh, Medea would have. "Very well then, Captain, Gamma Protocol initiated."

Nathan collapsed into the chair next to the console. "Continue trying to raise someone – anyone – on the planet. I need to know what's going on down there and what sort of assistance they can provide, or God forbid, we can provide them."

Something was wrong, terribly wrong. There was no way a ship as large as the *Argo* could enter orbit and someone from the surface not spot it. The *Argo* contained over twelve thousand men, women, and children within her stout hull. This also accounted for its crew, and the detachment of five hundred defense force soldiers assigned to provide internal security as well as serve as a protective force. She was the United World's first colony ship and was to have been mankind's greatest hope for continuation of the species. When the great disaster occurred and the oceans of Earth rose to claim most of its landmasses, the need to expand to the stars in order to survive had changed from an afterthought to a desperate gamble. Earth, it had been decided by the powers that be, could no longer support the human race as it once had. The rich and powerful, the military, and those with much needed talents and skills found shelter in the great island cities like Alantica, Pacifica and Lemura. Those less fortunate, who had survived the floods, were left to fend for themselves outside the massive protective walls as the Kaiju began to encroach further into human territory than ever before. Small enclaves fell before the might of the Mother Kaiju – towering, massive creatures who attacked any and all humans with single-minded drive.

The island city-states were, for all intents and purposes, military bases before the invasions began in earnest, or humanity wouldn't have stood a chance in those early days at all. Alantica and Pacifica were the two largest and best funded, with a work force that dwarfed the remaining bases, and through their combined efforts, the *Argo* was constructed in the safety of space next to the International Space Station. Even with humanity's continued existence on the line and a dedicated work force devoting all of its time and energy into construction, she took over a year to complete. Nathan knew that her being finished so fast was nothing short of a miracle, but those months had passed like years as he readied her crew and oversaw the work being done on her.

During the first stages of construction, the Kaiju attacks had been limited. One or two of the giant "Mother" Kaiju attacked a given city roughly every month, but as the Argo neared completion, the attacks began to increase. Mere weeks before he left the Earth's surface for the final time, a new breed of Kaiju had shown themselves. They weren't like the Mothers but were much smaller and faster. Their numbers seemed endless and they attacked with a frenzy mankind had not seen since the last world war. The "Dog" Kaiju, as the unfortunate infantry, which was tasked to fight them dubbed them, attacked the city-states en mass, armies of them swarming onto the beaches and overrunning any given base defenses. Many of the smaller city-states had been feeling the strain of defending against their relentless attacks, even as the *Argo's* main engines came fully online. The bloodbath at Nor-wic, Nathan recalled, had been especially horrific.

The slaughter of every man, woman and child at Nor-wic pushed the United World Council members into action. The new plan was simple. The *Argo* was to leave Earth's orbit and make her way to the Alpha Centauri system. It was a gamble, but a well-calculated one, and offered the best chance of finding a planet Earth-like enough to start over and rebuild. With her cargo loaded and the soon-to-be colonists safely aboard and in cryo-sleep, Nathan had stood on her bridge as space bent around her and she left the Sol System behind.

Unfortunately, even the best-laid plans have a tendency to go wrong.

Upon reaching Alpha Centauri, Nathan and a select few from the crew awoke to discover the sole planet close enough to Earth standards for a colony was already inhabited by a primitive race of bestial bipeds. These creatures were similar in appearance and behavior to the Sasquatch and yeti legends of Earth. Despite the firepower the *Argo* carried, it would have been impossible to wipe the monsters out completely and as long as they lived, there would be no peace on the new world.

Reluctantly, Nathan made the difficult call to return home to Earth. There was nothing for mankind in the Alpha Centauri system, and he felt the resources aboard the *Argo* could be better spent helping the whole of humanity fight the war with the Kaiju, than wasted randomly searching for a new home somewhere out in the stars.

Now, the *Argo* was home. *But what, if anything, had she come home to*, he wondered.

The visual images and recordings Medea had made of Pacifica Base flooded the screen in front of him, confirming that the city was gone. Thousands upon thousands of the lesser, smaller Dog Kaiju prowled its ruins and the shores surrounding the base. Nathan slumped back in his seat, stunned. So many lives lost. He had to wonder if anyone from Atlantica had survived down there when the Kaiju took the walls. He could only speculate on just how long it had taken the Kaiju to kill every last soul in the doomed city.

"Captain," Medea interrupted his musings. "Lemura Base will be within visual range in two minutes. Also, internal diagnostics are complete. Our communications relays are working at full capabilities. The problem, it seems, is on Earth."

"Thank you, Medea," Nathan grunted.

"And sir? I am sorry."

Nathan shook his head. He hadn't flown over 25 trillion miles to give up now. He pushed himself forward to sit up straighter. "Give me a wider scan, Medea. Someone has to be down there, and it's our job to find them. I want a search of *all* the bases, even the smaller ones."

*****

April "Kitty" Voecks rolled out of her cryo-bed, happy to be awake and for the pain to be gone. She rushed to don her uniform and get ready for action. The other members of the Argo's crew in her section were doing the same. They were all home now, and she was glad to be back, Kaiju war or no. Sure, she was disappointed about the mission's failure to find a habitable, safe world in the Alpha Centauri system. However, she had gotten to see the stars and travel among them. That had been her dream since she had been a child, a dream which she had lived at last.

She spotted Lieutenant Dale Fletcher staring at her as she zipped up her coveralls. She offered him an impish grin, which in turn caused him to blush fiercely. His brown hair was wild and hung down over to cover his forehead, though it did nothing for his current predicament. Officer or not, it was his trademark look, one that he was willing to skirt the regulations in order to keep. Despite his rough appearance, Fletcher was a very attractive man. Like her, he was in his mid-twenties, his body lean and hard from the training that came with being a part of the *Argo's* crew.

"Long trip for nothing, eh?" he managed to ask without stammering, brushing his hair up and out of his eyes.

"I wouldn't say that," Kitty laughed. "We've learned a lot about long-range space travel, and the *Argo* proved she's trustworthy. Plus, the astrophysics department learned more about the curvature of space-time around a binary star system."

"You have some crazy friends," Fletcher muttered.

"What? They showed me how light can be used to create energy," Kitty gushed. "Not just like solar energy, but how to actually *do* it! That was awesome!"

Fletcher shook his head. "You always look at the bright side of things."

"Did you mean to do that?" Kitty tittered. "I

find it's better than the alternative." Kitty flashed him another smile. "Got to get to my station, but I'll catch you later, okay?"

"You better," Fletcher said and dashed away in the opposite direction that she was heading. Kitty was a civilian sensor specialist, while Fletcher was part of the ship's engineering staff and thus, military. She would be needed on the ship's primary bridge as quickly as she could manage.

Kitty darted into a nearby lift and held its door for two more bridge crewmembers to enter. She found it more than a little strange that they did not have orders yet. When the *Argo* had dropped into normal space around Alpha Centauri, everything had been so rehearsed and planned out. Of course, she figured, no one had ever counted on them coming home. Things had not quite devolved into chaos, not yet. The *Argo's* crew was well trained at their jobs, but the air was filled with more than a little uncertainty. It seemed no one knew *exactly* what they should be doing. Everyone was just treating this as Alpha Centauri all over again, though the doubt of their actions showed in their expressions and movements. Steps were hesitant, and voices carried just a hint of unease in them. Earth was a known world, and likely Alantica or Pacifica had already checked in with the Captain to advise them on what came next. The *Argo* herself was too large and unwieldy to enter the Earth's atmosphere proper. There was always the threat they she'd break apart if she tried. That did not mean that people and supplies wouldn't start being shipped down as soon as possible.

The Captain of the *Argo* sat in the Argo's main control chair as she and the other two crew members accompanying her stepped off the lift and onto the bridge. Several others were already at their stations, waiting on the Captain's orders. Kitty hurried to her own and began to run the standard, post-voyage diagnostics on the sensor arrays as she had been trained to do. She glanced at the readings and blinked at the numbers. Something was not right here.

Commander Tiffanie Gray, the ship's communications officer, shot her a nervous glance. It was enough to let Kitty know that something was definitely up and whatever it was, it wasn't good. For the first time since she had been chosen for her job, she wished she hadn't been tasked to the bridge.

"Sensors online and operational, Captain," Kitty reported. She knew that the ship's AI would have had the sensors up and running long before she reached her post, but it was her job to verify that they were in working order. Even Medea could mess up, Kitty knew from training. After a few minutes of silence on the otherwise bustling bridge, Captain Whitmire stood. He tugged at his blouse and straightened out the wrinkles.

"Open a ship-wide channel," he ordered

Commander Gray. Kitty felt her heart skip a beat. The ship's AI could have done it for the Captain, but Medea's primary job was to guide the ship during the long journey across the stars when everyone was in cryo-sleep. Besides, Kitty knew from the last time she had been on the bridge, as advanced as Medea's programming was, the Captain always preferred a human being more. "This is Captain Nathan Alexander Whitmire speaking. At approximately, 0513 Zulu time, we achieved a stable orbit around Earth. Ladies and gentlemen, we are home."

Whitmire's words seemed to echo through out the corridors and various sections of the giant ship as Kitty listened to them, first hand, her station only a few yards from where he stood. She watched the Captain pause as Governor Jocker Trion came onto the bridge. Kitty's earlier sense of unease tripled on seeing the governor. She had only seen the woman one other time before, and that had been at the commissioning ceremony of the *Argo*. The governor exchanged a tense look with Captain Whitmire before he continued. "At this time, we have been unable to establish communications with the city of Alantica, or *any* of the other great city-states for that matter. It is with profound sadness that I must inform you that it has been confirmed that Alantica has fallen to the Kaiju, as have Pacifica and Lemura."

The following silence that spread across the bridge was deafening. The utter shock of the captain's words was nearly too much for Kitty to take in. Alantica... gone? It was like something out of a nightmare. She had grown up there, protected by the tall, massive walls and the loyal soldiers who patrolled the shores around it. She remembered the small candy shop around the corner from her parent's apartment and felt a small tear form in the corner of her eye as another positive memory of her childhood was ripped away from her. She sniffed slightly and rubbed her face. She had to put on a brave face for the rest of the crew. That was how everyone knew her to be – the perky, happy, cheerful civilian sensor technician. It was a role, everyone knew on the intellectual level, but Kitty knew that the facade helped.

"Unfortunately, the news I have to share with you gets no better," Whitmire went on. "During the time we were away, it appears the Kaiju won the war. Not a single city-state has answered our hails, small or large. Those Medea has been able to get detailed scans of thus far appear to have suffered the same fate as Alantica. Almost every land mass we've scanned so far is teeming with lesser Kaiju, except for Lemura. While that city-state remains silent as well, Nathan has detected power readings there that can only be of human origin. If there are survivors trapped within the fallen walls of Lemura, I feel it is our duty to take them in before we leave Earth once more. It's clear there is nothing for us here. Not anymore. Our home, our planet, is lost. End general transmission."

"So... that's it?" Ensign Hiro Iwakuma asked from the helm after a moment of absolute silence. "We're just going to leave, like that? Where will we go? What will we do?"

Kitty understood his concern and near panic. She felt something very similar threatening to well up from deep inside her. The calm emanating from Captain Whitmire, however, prevented the fear from overwhelming everyone on the bridge.

"That is our long-term plan, yes," Whitmire explained. "And Hiro? Remember your military bearing, son."

"Yes, sir!" Hiro snapped, his eyes locking back onto his duty station.

"But while we're here, we also need to resupply the ship and try to take aboard anyone left alive," Captain Whitmire continued. "It's our duty. All security and expeditionary personnel will be getting their orders shortly. As for the rest of us, we'll continue to learn what we can about what has happened here from orbit, as well as see if any of the orbital platforms remain functioning... though that seems unlikely at this time. Those platforms were built exclusively to support the ISS in the construction of the *Argo*, and were likely abandoned some time ago. Still, they're our best bet for refueling without endangering more of our personnel than need be."

*****

Lieutenant Jim McCoy sat in the aisle between the rows of lockers as the rest of his platoon was gearing up. Like most everyone else, he supposed he was in shock. Sure, it sucked that the mission had failed. But to come home to find the great cities of Earth gone? It simply was too much. So far, he was holding it together, if only by reminding himself that he was still alive. He guessed that this counted for something, especially when so many others were dead.

Corporal Steven Kirby slammed a fist into the door of his locker. Bright red blood smeared on the metal facing as he hit it again and again. "Damn it, Lieutenant, sir! What the crap are we supposed to do now?"

"Denting that locker isn't going to change anything," McCoy said without looking up from where he gazed at the *Argo's* cold metal floor. "You heard the Old Man's plan, like everyone else. We're Marines. Still are, despite the *security personnel* moniker they've hung on us to make the civvies more comfortable. But some things never change, and us doing our jobs is one of those things."

"Yeah, we bust in, save some civvies, load up, and bug out," Kirby growled. "Not much of a plan if you ask me."

"No one did, Kirby," McCoy pointed out.

"Even if we load back up to max," Private First Class Doug Grimes chimed in from a nearby locker, "the Argo can only hold so much. I mean, this ship has what, the storage space for maybe six months food and water? A bit longer maybe on the air with the scrubbers burning at maximum function and no breakdowns."

"You're right and you're wrong." McCoy stood. "That's six months for the entire population of the *Argo*. The Old Man's *not* going to wake the civvies or non-essential personnel we already got onboard. You can count on that. The newcomers will grab some of the reserve beds and we'll put them into cryo as well. Simple. It'll stretch things out by bunches, and give us more time."

"Time?!" Kirby snapped. "Time for what? All we'll be doing is waiting to die!"

"That's enough, Kirby," McCoy warned.

"I guess the LT means we'll be planet-hunting, Kirby. Right, sir?" Grimes turned to McCoy with a questioning expression.

"That's as good a guess as any," McCoy admitted after a moment. "To be honest, it may be the only thing we can do."

"The *Argo's* got the firepower to do some

serious damage," Kirby's voice was calmer now, but still tinged with hurt and anger.

"So what?" McCoy asked. "We can't take on an entire planet of Kaiju, Kirby. It's the same forsaken mess as Alpha Centauri was. Even if we somehow, by the grace of God and the *Argo's* weapons, pushed the blasted Kaiju back at one of the city-states, we couldn't hold it. Not for long, and not without constant resupply, which the *Argo*, I'm sad to say, cannot sustain."

"Four months," a deep, gravely voice sounded from behind them. Kirby and Grimes jumped slightly at the arrival of Gunnery Sergeant Jonny Iffland. "If you managed to take a city-state and found yourselves under constant siege, you may have four months before supplies run out. And that, ladies, is simple arithmetic. Ammunition kills Kaiju; food feeds Marines so that they have the strength to keep killing Kaiju. Take one away and you lose. Instead of whining and bitching about things, why don't you finish kitting yourselves out and get your asses down to the armory before I find something creative that needs to be cleaned. Understood?"

"Yes, Gunny!" Kirby and Grimes barked in unison and hurried out of the locker room.

"Thanks for the assistance, Gunny," McCoy told his senior non-commissioned officer.

"You had things well in order, sir," Iffland said in a respectful tone. "However, part of my job as your gunny is to make sure that the Marines are motivated and eager to do battle. I failed in my job, and for that I apologize, sir."

"Gunny, if anyone was excited about going on a suicide run to a dead world, I'd seriously question their sanity," McCoy announced.

"I'm excited as all get-out, sir," Iffland stated in a flat, bored tone. "I'm going to be the first Marine to combat-drop onto Earth from space, specifically into a potential warzone. Granted, I never thought that this would be after a failed colonization of a world inhabited by sasquatch-yeti things..."

"I'll meet you down in the armory." McCoy grinned and finished zipping up his coveralls. He walked out of the locker room and followed the Marines towards the armory.

Though the *Argo's* complement of troops numbered five hundred, the ship carried only a hundred and fifty suits of combat armor. The Dogkiller's battle armor was bulky things, and McCoy didn't really care for them. For all the sheer firepower they brought to the table, to him they felt like death traps. Every time he suited up, it felt more like getting into a coffin than a bipedal tank.

McCoy had spent a good portion of his life within the giant walls of Pacifica. He'd been born there to parents who were the average run-of-the-mill folks trying to make ends meet and get by in a world gone insane. When he came of age, he joined the Marines as fast as he could. The military offered a level of advancement and lifestyle he knew he never would have had a chance at. His unit was immediately shipped off to Atlantica, and he never saw his family again. Sometimes, he regretted that, others not so much. He had a new family now, the one he had chosen. When word of the *Argo's* construction got out to the public, McCoy had done everything he could to make sure he would be on it when it left Earth. That, he didn't regret at all.

*****

Captain Whitmire laid the data pad on his desk, looking up as Kitty and Tiffanie entered his briefing room. They were both extremely nervous and apprehensive; it was easy to see.

"Take a seat," he gestured at the chairs in front of his desk. The two women did as he instructed. Once they were settled in, he continued. "I'm sorry to have called you away from your duties. I realize there is a lot going on right now, but I have need of your particular set of skills. Kitty, you're the best civilian sensor tech onboard the *Argo*. Your aptitude skills are off the charts, and you far exceed the physical standards set forth by the security forces. And Diana, you're the ranking communications officer. As I am sure you both already know, the orbital stations around Earth were abandoned once we left the system, just as we feared they would be. They've either been abandoned and scavenged, or their orbits became unstable and they eventually fell from the sky."

"That's correct, sir," Kitty ventured. "Scans of those on this side of the planet with us show no life-forms aboard any of the ones still in the air."

"And I still can't raise any of the others on any frequency," Tiffanie added.

"One of the stations still seems to have power," Whitmire said with a glance at Kitty, who nodded. "Tango Zeta 3, actually. It is rather close to our current position, which is extremely fortuitous. I am sending over a small detachment of engineers, along with a platoon of security personnel to salvage what they can from it. But what I really want is that station's logs. I, for one, want a clearer picture of what happened while we were gone. Those logs could tell us a lot about the fate of those we left behind on Earth, as well as help us to decide the course of action we need to take next."

"But I thought you had decided that already, sir," Tiffanie shifted in her seat uncomfortably.

"To a degree, the governor and I already have," Whitmire admitted, "but in our current situation, a lot could change on extremely short notice. If the logs are encrypted with newer codes than those we are currently using and others escaped Earth besides us, or the station's systems have suffered damage and any messages left for us are recoverable, you two are the best chance I have at getting my hands on that data. However, neither of you have any field experience, and I know that this is far outside your normal job. It's why I'm asking for a volunteer."

"I'll go," Kitty said after a moment. Tiffanie looked relieved as Whitmire nodded.

"Good," he said. "I was hoping it would be you, no offense to the commander. This was not a choice I wanted to make for either of you. Get your gear together. The three shuttles leaving for Tango Zeta 3 will be heading out in less than hour."

"Yes sir!" Kitty replied. "I'll be ready."

*****

Grimes vomited onto the floor of the transport, the foul-smelling remnants of his breakfast splashing against the metal floor. None of it landed on the young soldier, which McCoy found surprising. Not an easy task with the safety harnesses that he and the other members of First and Second squads wore. The five-point metal harness was designed to prohibit movement and prevent injury, and turning one's head to vomit was supposed to be impossible.

Entry into the Earth's atmosphere was a bumpy

ride. The entire shuttle shook and vibrated as it descended towards the planet's surface. It came as no surprise to McCoy that the younger soldiers, who had never been forced to be airborne qualified, found the violent movements of the shuttle to be nauseating. He glanced over at Grimes and saw the poor kid had begun to dry heave, his stomach now empty. He'd considered ordering everyone to not eat before dropping, but considering that it had been well over a year since anyone had eaten a thing, he decided against it.

McCoy still felt bad for the younger soldier, though. His own stomach churned and gurgled nervously, but he had been airborne qualified back when it had meant something. He also had been part of the initial drop onto Alpha Centauri Prime, and felt that he was ready for the new hell they were about the enter. He looked around the bay at the rest of the men. He knew precisely how many of them had made a combat drop before, which was not many. Still, he had confidence in his men.

The wild bucking of the shuttle eased as they passed through the turbulence at long last. The shuttle pilot's voice came over the shared comm link of both squad's combat helmets. "ETA in five."

"You heard the man, ladies," the Gunny barked. "This is gonna be the best day of your young, pathetic lives. Tell me how good it's gonna be!"

"Damn good!" the two squads chorused loudly.

"How good?" the Gunny asked.

"So good it hurts!" the squads finished. More than a few of them were grinning now. McCoy hid a small smile of his own. While he was in overall command of the drop, he had worked with the Gunny for a long time and trusted his senior NCO explicitly. The Gunny, he knew from experience, knew the men better than anyone.

As soon as the shuttle touched down, its rear door sprang open and the safety harnesses snapped open. The Gunny led the squads out onto the beach just outside the main entrance to the city of Lemura. McCoy followed on his heels, but froze in his tracks only feet outside of the shuttle. The walls of the great city were scarred, with entire sections of them collapsed. The beach around the shuttle was covered in the skeletons of lesser Dog Kaiju and rusting, damaged suits of combat armor. McCoy didn't recognize the design of the suits, but could easily see the lethality in their design lines. They were like sleeker versions of the Dogkillers, the two armored squads they would be linking up with would be wearing, but better armed and technologically advanced. He wished for a moment that he had these suits at his disposal instead of his standard armor.

McCoy's own two squads were pure infantry. No Dogkiller armor for them. Captain Whitmire had deemed it would be best to have some troops on the ground that could go places which the bulky Dogkiller suits might not be able. McCoy often suspected that Whitmire was a traditionalist like himself when it came to all the high tech toys the army and navy had at their disposal these days.

"Now this," the Gunny whistled softly, "this was a *battle*, boys."

McCoy spotted the two squads of eight Dogkiller-clad troopers clamoring towards their position. "I want Dogkillers on point and bringing up the rear of the column as we advance into the city. Gunny, form us up."

"Let's move, boys! Hup-hup-hup!"

The strange power readings that they had been sent to investigate were deep inside the city. Captain Whitmire had theorized that they might be coming from some sort of last resort, a safe and hidden bunker. If that was the case, getting into it might be an issue, but that was one McCoy could deal with if they found it.

The problem at hand was making it through the city itself. There was no doubt it would be teeming with Dog Kaiju, and the scans taken by the shuttle crew on the way down suggested that, while there were clear paths to avoid them, these changed, and the soldiers would have little warning should that happen.

However, aside from the legions of corpses covering the beach, not even one had been spotted thus far. McCoy knew that the monsters could be crafty when they had to be, but this? This bordered on the ridiculous. Usually, if a Dog Kaiju caught wind of humans, they came running. The noisy, heavy, lumbering Dogkillers should have been a dinner bell for the beasts. Yet none came as the Dogkillers led the way. Their internal motors whined as they clanked about, guns ready, moving towards the city.

The sun was setting on the horizon, its dying rays gleaming on the splashing waves of the water. The stench of *so* many bodies decaying in the heat of the waning day was simply too much. He saw one of the regular infantry under his command stop and throw up next to a ruined wall. McCoy felt the gorge rising in his belly as well, but swallowed it down. He wondered if the men and women inside the Dogkillers could smell it as well.

The column marched into the city proper and began to move along its streets. McCoy directed its movement from the column's center using a high-powered, handheld sensor unit. According to its readings, the power signatures they were seeking lay around three miles to the north. He checked their surroundings, but the deep shadow cast by the setting sun created a lot of false pits and hid obstacles from them. The column slowed as the infantry began to pick its way through the rubble more slowly.

"Kaiju!" McCoy heard someone scream over the comm link. The world around him exploded into chaos as Dog Kaiju came pouring out of the alleyways, side streets, and the ruins of Lemura all around the four squads. The heavy weapons of the Dogkiller troopers rang out like the thunder of a summer storm, scything the Dogs down as the armored soldiers clustered together to protect their flanks. The chattering of automatic small arms fire was quickly added to the noise as the two infantry squads joined in.

It was impossible for McCoy to get an accurate guess at the number of lesser Kaiju they were facing from his position, but he could see enough to know they were all royally fubared. The Kaiju had to number at least in the hundreds and the noise of the battle would surely draw any others nearby down on them too. Their window of safe passage had been slammed shut on their fingers, and now, his sole focus changed to keeping the men and women under his command alive.

McCoy watched as one of the large Dogkiller suits spun to bring its main weapon up at an approaching Kaiju. The weapon's blast tore the Kaiju to pieces in mid-air, leaving nothing larger than a kernel of corn behind. McCoy realized that the soldier in the suit must have switched the type of rounds his weapon was using, because after that first deafening blast, a stream of high velocity rounds erupted from its barrel. The trooper swept his weapon back and forth, pouring concentrated fire into the front ranks of the charging Kaiju. The creatures caught in its fury danced and twitched as the rounds ripped through their scaly flesh. Geysers of Kaiju blood erupted from their bodies which splattered all over the street and coated the ruined walls of the fallen city. The ground beneath McCoy's feet shook as a thermobaric grenade someone had lobbed into the swarms of Kaiju detonated. A nearby building, already teetering, fell over and wiped out a large group of Kaiju that had been moving up behind them.

The squads were collapsing in on each other, their formations growing tighter as the Kaiju forces pressed down on them. Dog Kaiju died by the dozens in their frenzied bid to kill and devour the humans before them. McCoy watched one of the creatures flop over and lie still, long strands of its intestines spilling out of its abdomen around it. Another of the Kaiju came barreling at him, managing to close to a relatively short distance without being cut down by the withering hail of gunfire from the soldiers. He whipped up his rifle and emptied half its magazine into the thing before it finally died, a snarl still on its lips. The Dog Kaiju came tumbling to a stop less than two yards from where he stood. McCoy knew the squads needed to fall back to a more secure location, but there was nowhere for them to go. They were surrounded, cut off and alone on this desolate Hell which had once been his birthplace, fighting to hold what little ground they still had.

The shuttles, he thought. They had lifted as soon as the squads were deployed, but were supposed to be on stand-by somewhere above the city, waiting to be called in for extraction. "Phoenix Flight, this is Lion Six. We need air support at our present location!" McCoy yelled over the comm. "Phoenix Flight, I need you to do your best impersonation of an artillery barrage. Relaying coordinates to you now!"

"Lion Six, this is Phoenix Two... sir, that's right on top of you!" a stunned voice answered him.

"You don't think I know that? Do it now, damn you!" McCoy snarled as he emptied the other half of his magazine into a Kaiju that jumped past one of the Dogkillers and made a beeline for him. His steady stream of gunfire met the thing head-on. Rounds raked across its chest, sending chunks of meat and muscle flying. Bergman sidestepped the Kaiju's corpse as it crashed to the ground, coming to a rest in the spot where he had been standing moments before. He ejected his rifle's spent magazine, slamming a fresh one into the weapon as he heard the shuttles beginning their approach. Their engines howled above the cacophony of weapons fire and snarls around him. He took a deep breath before shouting, "Y'all want to get your faces *on the ground right fucking now!*"

*****

Kitty watched the Tango Zeta 3 station growing larger on the small screen of her handheld sensor unit. Hacking into the main sensor feed of the shuttle she was aboard was an easy thing, and she had wanted to watch the group's approach first hand. She sat in the shuttle's rear compartment with several other techs and a small cluster of six, heavily armed soldiers. They were there to watch over the technicians and provide security, just in case.

"Having fun?" a familiar voice asked. It was Fletcher, sneaking a peek at the small sensor screen from over her shoulder.

She killed the feed, powering down the device. It wasn't against regulations to do what she had done, but it wasn't exactly something that would be looked on favorably either. Regulations aside, she did want to save her battery on the device, especially if they were going to be on the station for more than an hour or two.

"Not really," she answered gruffly. Fletcher's laughter made her relax in spite of everything going on around them. "You better get strapped in," she told him as she patted the seat next to her own. "We'll be docking soon."

"Yes, ma'am," Fletcher smiled and into the seat.

Kitty let the silence envelope her as she tilted her head back and stared at the ceiling of the shuttle. Her mind drifted back to the schematics of the station they were approaching and she wondered what they would find there. After a few minutes of silence, she felt Fletcher's eyes on her. She pointedly ignored him and tried to settle her nerves.

"This is your first time out, isn't it?" Fletcher asked in a quiet voice. "I mean, since we left Earth's surface."

Kitty craned her head around to glare at him. "And I imagine you have a *lot* of experience with this kind of thing, huh, Mr. Engineering?"

"More than you would think," he answered, his tone sincere. "Trust me, this is nothing compared to a space walk across the *Argo's* hull to fix some damaged plating on her belly."

"I guess not," Kitty allowed with a slight smile. "I bet that is pretty messed up, getting up and down mixed up, not sure where things end and where everything begins."

"And beautiful," Fletcher admitted. "If you can get past the whole *what if my mag boots lose their lock on the hull and I go drifting off to die* thing."

The shuttle around them rocked as a loud *clang* ran throughout and along the length of its hull. The steady thrum of the engines, which had been a constant throughout their short journey, dropped to almost nothing. The spacecraft grew very silent for a moment, with only the steady hiss of the oxygen scrubbers to be heard. The murmur of the pilots broke up that monotony, and the noise in the shuttle grew back to their previous levels as everyone began to talk at once.

"And we're docked," Fletcher said, flipping the release of the safety harness he'd donned at Kitty's request. Kitty did the same and started to get up. Fletcher placed a hand on her arm, stopping her. He gestured at the soldiers behind them with his free hand. "Don't get in such a rush. Those guys will go in first. It's their job to secure to the place before folks like us get to go in."

Blushing, Kitty shifted in her seat. She felt like a total newbie for not thinking of that herself. She blamed her nerves, but still that was no excuse for an experienced individual of her pay grade. It didn't matter to her if she had experience in *this* kind of thing or not. The bridge could be an intense pressure cooker of stress and hard situations where one wrong move could cost the lives of hundreds, if not the *Argo* itself. Letting something as simple as docking with a station shake her up was inexcusable the way she saw things.

"Sorry," she told Fletcher. "I suppose I'm a bit on edge."

"Forget about it," he shrugged off her apology.

"If I said I wasn't wound a bit tight myself, I'd be lying. Now just sit back for a minute and let the guys with the guns earn their pay, okay? Besides, it's not like we really have anything to worry about. We aren't going to find any Kaiju waiting for us up here. The worst we're likely to run in to are some emaciated corpses, and if we're lucky, the guys with guns will cover those up long before we even go over to Tango Zeta 3. It's those poor soldiers who got sent to Earth that are in real trouble."

Kitty nodded, powering up her handheld sensor again. She began to play around with its controls as the first of the troops left the soldiers and made their way across the airlock into Tango Zeta 3. She had a job to do, and it would be completely unacceptable for her to be unprepared for the task at hand.

*****

When the wave of fire and heat ended, McCoy found himself lying face down in the street. He shook his head to clear it and saw both of the assault shuttles veering upwards and gaining altitude as they sped clear. A small part of him knew that they would resume their over-watch from above the ruined city, but the comfort was fleeting at best. Smoke filled the air about him and piles of burning Kaiju bodies lay around his position. The airstrike had been borne of desperation, but appeared to have worked and bought them some breathing room.

"Sound off!" he ordered as he scurried to his

feet. As the survivors of the squads with him called out to report in, more Kaiju were coming. He could see the cursed things running along the streets towards them in the distance, jumping over the bodies of their fallen brothers in their eagerness to kill them. He dumped the data of the location of the power signature they were headed for into the main combat link he and the other squad members shared. He hoped that the Dogkiller suits were coherent enough to understand his orders. "Rally at those coordinates! Third Squad, provide cover. First, Second, move your butts! Fourth Squad, clear a path!"

The squads spread out, guns blazing, as they moved northward. Fourth Squad – Dogkiller troops – began to fire, their massive weapons cutting deep grooves into the front lines of the Kaiju masses that were forming up and attempting to stop their progression. Everyone else took random pot shots at the Kaiju coming in at them from the side streets and alleys, but their main focus was on hauling butt. McCoy prayed that whatever they found at the locator beacon would be both defensible and worth it. They couldn't stay out in the open as they were, or they would be overrun and torn apart by the sheer mass of the Dog Kaiju.

"Some days it just doesn't pay to get out of bed, does it, sir?" the Gunny asked as sidled up to McCoy. "Ryan! Check your six, corporal!"

The Dogkiller in question turned with

impressive speed, but it was not nearly fast enough. Five of the Dog Kaiju latched onto his armor, their combined weight throwing him off balance. Ryan managed to grab one by the neck. The power of the servos in the suit's hand crushed the thing's throat as his fingers closed around it. The monsters were in too close for him to use the suit's weapon effectively, McCoy realized. Sparks flew where razor-like claws struck metal, as one of the Kaiju delivered a glancing blow to Ryan's armored head. McCoy heard Ryan cursing over the comm link and knew that the Kaiju had damaged the suit. While the Dogkiller suits were sealed systems, with their own internal environment, a damaged helmet could leave the soldier inside blind and deaf to the outside world.

Sure enough, McCoy recognized the signs of a complete systems failure as Ryan's Dogkiller stumbled backwards, arms flailing in the air. It toppled over with a loud *thud* on the street. Cracks formed and spider webbed out from the point of its impact. One of the Kaiju lost a leg to the combat suit's heavy weight, tearing its own limb off as the Kaiju tried to free itself.

McCoy paused and took careful aim with his rifle. He steadily applied pressure to the trigger with his finger, and the rifle bucked slightly as he put a round into the monster's head. It sprawled out on the pavement, a gaping hole between its eyes, and a pool of blood growing around the stump of its lower thigh. That was the only help McCoy could offer

Ryan at the time, though. If he stayed in one spot, he was as good as dead. The Kaiju were swarming like sharks in a frenzy, the scent of blood filling the air and the gunfire and noise of the Dogkillers continuing to draw the terrifying little beasties out. McCoy knew that Ryan wouldn't be getting up without the help of a crane or four other Dogkillers. The heavy, older model Dogkillers, once down, were nearly impossible to get upright again. He saw the remaining three Kaiju on top of Ryan, ripping away plating from his suit as they tried to get at him. It was just a matter of time until they did. Even if Ryan managed to fight off the three, more would take their places and his damaged suit wouldn't up to the task of stopping them. There were no other Dogkillers available to help up their fallen comrade. It was painful for McCoy to watch another soldier under his command slowly opened up by Kaiju like a rusted old can of sardines.

The flash and thunder of a second thermobaric grenade exploding caught McCoy by surprise. The blast's shockwave picked him up and threw him several yards. He twisted his body like a contortionist and somehow managed to hit the street rolling. He sprang to his feet as a snarling Kaiju plowed into him. The strength behind the monster's impact sent him flying again. He landed on his back with a grunt, his breath knocked from his lungs. He wheezed, trying to force air back in as he raised his weapon at the Kaiju looming over him. The barrel managed to line up with the Kaiju's chest long enough for the lieutenant to get a clean shot. He yanked back on the trigger, ignoring every firing discipline he'd ever learned in his life. McCoy kept his trigger pulled tight as he sprayed dozens of rounds into the Kaiju at point-blank range. The rounds cut their way into the Kaiju's stomach, shredding it, pieces of its organs and intestinal track flying from its twitching body. He lashed out with his legs, violently kicking the thing's collapsing corpse away from him as it fell flat onto the ruined street.

"LT!" a voice shouted over the comm link of his helmet. He faintly recognized Kirby's voice. "We've reached the target! It's a bunker of some kind!"

"Can you get into it?" McCoy asked, getting to his feet. He dumped the empty magazine onto the street and slapped a fresh one in.

"Yes sir! It looks as if a Mother Kaiju had a go at trying to dig into it. A good portion of the bunker is exposed including its main door," Kirby replied, the excitement evident to McCoy over the comm channel. McCoy motioned at the Gunny, who waved in reply and came trotting over. Kirby continued to chatter into the comm. "Grimes was able to get the door open. We're inside and holding, but the entrance isn't large enough to get the Dogkillers inside! They've formed up and created an external defensive perimeter right outside the door. So far, it's keeping the Dogs off us, but I don't know how much longer they can hold! We need some support, sir!"

"Let's move, people!" Gunny shouted, his bellow cutting through the sounds of battle like a knife. The surviving squads began to move, slowly at first, but with greater confidence as the Dog Kaiju were pushed back by the combined firepower of the four squads.

McCoy rounded a corner in the street and the battle for the bunker came into view. The remaining three Dogkiller suits were fighting for their lives, their main guns turning waves of incoming Kaiju to pulp. Kirby and Grimes stood in the doorway of the bunker, adding fire from their rifles to the bloodbath that was taking place around the half-buried structure. The bunker itself looked like a giant metal box, six feet or so below street level. The claw marks of a massive Mother Kaiju stretched across the whole area from where the beast had been trying to dig into it. McCoy hoped that Mother Kaiju was long gone, because there was not a hope in Hell for them if she was lingering about.

McCoy didn't slow as he approached the entrance to the bunker. He dove, barreling passed the two soldiers as he headed for the open door, the Gunny hot on his tail. Kirby and Grimes stopped firing as they moved to allow him inside. McCoy clambered to his feet and began to fire into the mass of Kaiju to cover the remaining troop's entrance into the bunker.

The shock of seeing no one else alive out there almost caused him to stop shooting. He blinked for a moment, stunned, before he looked over at Kirby.

"Get that door closed!" McCoy roared. Kirby stared at him in disbelief.

"But sir, the Dogkillers..." Kirby started to say. The Gunny pushed past him and grabbed the door's controls.

"Nothing we can do for them, son," the Gunny said, not unkindly, as he activated the door's controls. "They can't fit in here, and if we leave the door open, our mission has failed. And boys? This mission cannot fail."

As the five-ton, titanium-reinforced door began to slide close, McCoy watched one of the last Dogkiller suits fall. A larger-than-normal Dog Kaiju jumped through the air at it, taking its armored head clean from the armor's shoulders with a single swipe of its clawed and scaly hand. Kaiju eyes, filled with hate and rage, met McCoy's human ones for a brief instant. The lieutenant felt a cold shiver strike deep into his soul as the door clanged shut.

*****

"Please understand, ma'am, that the secondary team hasn't swept through everything yet," Sergeant Tim Fishlock told Kitty as she stepped out of the airlock onto Tango Zeta 3. "We've done a rough and tumble recon of this station, but... well, ma'am, there's some weird stuff over here. Stuff I've never seen before to be honest with you."

Fletcher stood beside Kitty, his engineering kit in hand. He had been ready to enter the station, but now paused at the sergeant's words. He shot a concerned look at Kitty, who was looking past the sergeant's bulky frame and into the station. She blinked and looked back up at the large soldier.

"What exactly do you mean by 'weird stuff'?"

"According to Captain Whitmire's orders, you're the ranking individual here, ma'am. Maybe it would be best if you took a look for yourself," Fishlock said, obviously relieved to pass the responsibility over to someone else. "Yeop, Greenwood, get over here!"

Two of Fishlock's men rushed over at the sound of his booming voice.

"Sergeant, I really don't think..." Kitty's voice trailed off as Fishlock turned a steely eye on her.

"Escort the lady and her friend to that mess in the aft section," Fishlock ordered. "You know the one I'm talking about."

"Sergeant? You said we didn't–" Yeop began to protest but quickly cut himself off. He nodded

43

briskly. "Roger that. Ma'am, sir, if you'll follow us?"

"Um, actually," Fletcher looked sheepishly at the sergeant. "I really need to get to engineering. I need to make sure the power and life support are going to stay on while we're here."

"Fine," Fishlock answered in a stressed-out tone. "You're with me then."

"This way, ma'am," Yeop said, leading Kitty deeper into the station as Fishlock and Fletcher turned and walked down another passageway into another part of Tango Zeta 3. Greenwood followed Kitty and Yeop closely, his rifle, like Yeop's held at the ready. While neither soldier had his finger on the trigger, they were close enough to doing so to make the civilian mildly perturbed.

"You guys seem a bit nervous," Kitty said and made a small motion at their rifles. "Is there something going on that I need to know about?"

"Don't you worry about a thing, ma'am," Greenwood told her. "We got you covered."

Along the path to wherever it was Yeop and Greenwood were taking her, Kitty noticed strange markings and damage to the walls of the station's corridors. What appeared to be a fine layer of rust coated the walls in random spots, creating a patchwork look all throughout. Here and there, they would pass a mangled corpse lying on the floor and blocking their route, which Yeop would nudge aside with his boot as gently as he could manage. The bodies were in a strange state of decomposition; as if something onboard the station had accelerated their decay rate, while allowing the membrane to remain mostly intact across the body. That alone was very strange. Decomposition was a tricky thing to gauge in an artificial environment like the Tango Zeta 3 station, but it didn't take a doctor to see that something was very wrong with the corpses. Their skin was dried and withered, as one would expect from a body that was not subjected to any form of humidity. However, even her untrained eye could see that there was a distinct and disturbing rot beneath it all.

"What in the world happened here?" Kitty asked, though she had a nagging sensation that she didn't really want to know.

"Not a clue, ma'am," Yeop admitted. "Our corpsman said it wasn't like anything he had ever seen. Honestly, we were hoping that Captain Whitmire would give us a few doctors, biologists, or something. He didn't send over any med techs, just you and a whole bunch of engineering types. Guess he didn't figure on anything over here being out of the ordinary."

"You said your corpsman hadn't seen anything like it before?" Kitty looked around. "Where is he now?"

"Hold one, ma'am," Yeop said and clicked his comm. "PO Esper, report to Delta Checkpoint."

A minute later, a short, squat man of indeterminate age ambled into the corridor. He gave Kitty a curt nod before he looked over at Yeop. "What's up, Corporal?"

"Tell Ms. Kitty here exactly what you told me," Yeop said. The corpsman blinked, confused.

"I don't know what to say, Corporal," Esper said. "I said it wasn't like anything I'd ever seen before–"

"Before that," Yeop cut him off. The shorter man's face paled.

"That was just me running my mouth, Corporal," Esper protested. "I didn't mean it."

"Tell her anyway," Yeop ordered. Esper sighed.

"I said that it looked like those experiments I read about during the Second World War," the corpsman explained at last. "You know, the ones that the Nazis ran on the Jews, and what the Japanese did to the Chinese? Just... some really messed up crap, ma'am. Inhumane. But it reminded me of some mad scientist's experiments, but on a level that's gonna give me nightmares for the rest of my life."

Kitty was beginning to wish that she hadn't volunteered to come over to the station. "Looks like he's right about that," Kitty agreed. She knelt over a nearby corpse and whipped out her pocket sensor. She ran it over the head and neck portion of the corpse, but the results were inconclusive. She frowned and moved the sensor down. The result was the same.

Her knowledge of biology was very limited, though she knew enough to recognize that whatever had happened to the corpse on the ground was not a natural occurrence. She pushed the sensor closer to the body and tried to get a better reading. The sensors flickered for a moment before data began to stream across the small screen.

Kitty's eyes tracked the information for a moment before she began to nod. The sensor would need a few minutes to process her findings, but it wasn't immediately dangerous, whatever it was. She put the sensor away and looked up at the three soldiers standing nearby.

"This is fascinating," Kitty said. "Thanks for bringing this to my attention."

"This wasn't what we wanted to show you, ma'am," Yeop shook his head. "This is... a smaller part of what we found."

"There's more?" Kitty asked, eyes wide.

"It gets much, much worse, ma'am," Esper said. "You have a strong stomach?"

"I can hold my own," Kitty proclaimed.

"Good enough for me," Yeop said and motioned towards a door at the end of the corridor. "Greenwood, Esper, escort the lady down the hall."

"You're not coming?" Kitty asked, surprised.

"Rank hath its privileges, ma'am," Yeop said. "I don't want to see that mess anymore than I need to."

Kitty glared at him, not sure what to make of his warning or reticence. She followed the soldiers down to the aforementioned door and pulled her sensor unit out again. Kitty stretched it out in front of her. The bio-readings on the other side of the smashed door were off the chart with activity, but nothing showed as a real life form, at least not in the sense of a human or Kaiju. The data was there, but much like the corpse she had inspected moments before, the results of the data were inconclusive. Gathering her courage, Kitty walked to the doorway and peered into the room.

"God have mercy on us all," she breathed as her eyes took in the mass of living, writhing tissue that covered the room's floor and dangled from its ceiling. The whole place was alive with a slime-slicked flesh that moved and oozed about like flowing blood. It moved like one organism, pulsing and throbbing in a peculiar beat. It was flesh, and yet it was not. The sensors began to go crazy as it began to pick up dangerous biologically hazardous readings in the room. She gagged as the smell hit her nose. Kitty took a step back away from the door. "Burn it. Burn it all. Now!"

Half an hour later, the room had been cleared. Fishlock's men had sealed it and torched the mess inside with improvised flamethrowers taken from the Tango Zeta 3 station's own arsenal. Yeop, it seemed, was an amateur pyromaniac who was able to whip up three flamethrowers from an old welding kit, leftover fuels and a few pressure valves. Kitty ordered all the bodies littering the station disposed of as well. They were gathered up by soldiers in bio-gear and jettisoned into space. Kitty had one of the soldiers collect a small sample of the stuff from inside the room before it was burnt. She kept it, along with her own sensor readings, to take back to the *Argo* for someone more qualified to take a look at. Only then did she return to her original mission aboard Tango Zeta 3.

Yeop and Greenwood stayed with her as she headed for the station's bridge and began the long process of hacking into and downloading the sensor and comm logs. After another hour of cursing and futility, she managed to crack it. She felt like ripping her hair out once she was in, though. Just as the Captain had feared, the station's encryptions were more advanced and based off a completely different algorithm than the ones being used aboard the *Argo*. Kitty still managed to gain some access to them, though, and got what little of the data she could pull secured for transport back. She could've started plowing through it all right there if she had wanted, but Kitty wasn't staying on the station any longer than she *had* to. For all she knew, she and the entire group had been exposed to whatever had killed the station's crew and created the fleshy mass on the station. They would all need to go through a long decontamination shower and be held in isolation before being allowed return to the *Argo* proper.

It was going to be a very dull three days, she knew.

*****

Nathan sat alone in his briefing room. The news seemed to be getting worse with every passing hour the *Argo* maintained orbit around Earth. Though the *Argo* was still in communication with the two Phoenix combat shuttles on Earth, she had lost contact with the remnants of the force still on the ground. The shuttle pilots only knew that the unit had came under heavy Kaiju attack, which they had provided air cover for, while the soldiers attempted to regroup. Just as quickly as the Kaiju attack had begun, the comms of the men on the ground went silent, as though something had simply cut off their signals at the source. The captain's gut told him not to give up on the unit just yet. McCoy was in charge down there, and the man had a knack for pulling off miracles and keeping people alive.

When the shuttles he had dispatched to Tango Zeta 3 station returned, he had hoped for a brief instance that they'd bring some insight with them into what happened on Earth while the *Argo* was gone. Answers were in short supply, though. To make matters worse, it was possible that the entire team that he had sent over to the station had been exposed to some sort of biological outbreak. He had been forced to send them all into isolation, and now Kitty and the others sat in individual decontamination chambers awaiting their fate. Assuming they hadn't brought back something lethal with them that would tear through the *Argo's* inhabitants like wildfire, it would still be days, at a minimum, until he could get Kitty to parse over the data on the bridge where he could watch over her shoulder. Still, it wasn't a complete loss. He had ordered that she be allowed to work on sorting through it all, while she was in isolation, but even so, it wasn't quite as good as having a full system, such as her normal duty station on the bridge.

In truth, the *only* good news he had received was the confirmation that the station contained the fuel that the Argo sorely needed for eventual departure from Earth's orbit and their subsequent search for a new home. That, too, would take hours to transfer all the fuel over to the *Argo*, but at least it was good to know the fuel was there for the taking.

If he had to risk, or even sacrifice, a few dozen crewmembers to get it onboard, then he would not hesitate to do so. A few dozen lost in order to save the other thousands of souls on the *Argo* that remained in cryo-sleep was more than a fair trade. Humanity had to survive somehow.

Nathan got up from behind his desk and paced back and forth across the open portion of the room. He hated waiting with a resolute passion, but at the moment, it seemed that was all there was to do. Nathan changed his path as a thought struck him. He headed for the large observation window behind his desk. Not a true window but a computer monitor from which he could see a perfectly rendered Earth as the cameras saw it, it was still close enough or him to often forget that it was just a projection. He stood in front of it and stared out at the planet below. Gone were the luscious greens and whites colors on the planet's surface from the days before the Kaiju War. Twisted shades of grays and unnaturally deep blues replaced them, making the world appear as dead as the race that had once dominated the top of its food chain.

His intercom buzzed suddenly, interrupting his musings. He grumbled and acknowledged receipt.

"Sir!" Tiffanie called over the comm system. "You're needed on the bridge!"

"On my way," Nathan answered, while taking one final, lingering look at the changed and decimated planet below that the human race had once called home. His home. His birthplace and, for the billions of souls left behind, a mass grave. He wondered just how history would record the event.

Assuming that there would be anyone around to write it, at least.

He stepped onto the bridge. Tiffanie stood at the sensor station next to Yamilé, the young woman who had taken over for Kitty during her forced absence. From the looks on their faces, he could easily guess that whatever it was they needed him for, it wasn't going to be good news.

"What is it?" Nathan snapped as he walked over to where the duo was stationed. He instantly regretted his tone.

"Captain, the sensors are picking a massive geothermic and tectonic disruption in the southeast area of where Pacifica once stood," Yamilé said hastily, as if she were unsure of herself and the readings. "Coming from... eighteen kilometers from beneath the surface."

"And that means?" he asked. "An earthquake?"

"Erupting volcanoes, earthquakes, wide-spread seabed disruptions," Tiffanie explained. "It's like the entire ocean bed in that area is tearing itself apart."

"That's where the Mariana Trench was, isn't it?" Yamilé wondered aloud.

"I don't see why this concerns us," Nathan said. "Earth has always been seismically active, even after the events precluding to the Kaiju War. Especially in *that* area. The Ring of Fire, remember? Besides, we're leaving as soon as things are resolved with the team on Lemura. Focus on your job."

"It's like nothing the sensors have ever seen before, sir," Yamilé told him. Tiffanie nodded as Yamilé continued explaining. "The affected area is hundreds of miles wide or larger. I don't know how to explain it exactly, but it's as if the entire Pacific Plate is tearing itself apart down there."

Nathan sighed and rubbed his temples. "Is the disturbance close enough to affect our team down in Lemura?"

"No sir," Yamilé answered. "Not unless it gets bigger and kicks off the biggest tsunami mankind has ever seen."

"Then take all the readings you want for scientific proposes, I suppose, but don't bother me with it again unless it becomes a more direct concern to our team on Lemura.   Understood?"

"Yes, Captain," Yamilé answered glumly, clearly disappointed with his reaction to her discovery.

*****

"What the Hell is this place?" McCoy asked as he and Grimes walked slowly through the twisting system of corridors inside the bunker. He ran a hand along the concrete walls and whistled.

"Don't look a gift horse in the mouth, sir" Grimes said. "I'm just glad its door appears to be holding. If not for that door, sir, we'd all be dead."

McCoy shook his head. "I don't think we have to worry too much about that now. You saw the outside of this place, right? A bloody Mother Kaiju couldn't get in here, and not for lack of trying."

"I bet, if given more time, it could have," Grimes argued. "I'd guess something drove or lured it away before it could get in, sir."

"Quit harassing the lieutenant, Grimes," Gunny Iffland growled, as he appeared from the depths of another corridor. "Get with Sergeant Frandsen and make sure that the door stays secured. Find Kirby and see if he's found anything useful in this place. Food, ammo, anything that can help."

"Roger that, Gunny," Grimes said and trotted back towards the big blast door. The Gunny pinched the bridge of his nose and sighed.

"Gotta quit letting them argue with you, sir," he said. "They start questioning your orders, they stop listening."

"I know, Gunny," McCoy nodded. "It's rough sometimes, seeing these kids scared like this and trying to keep them alive and functioning."

"With all due respect, sir, that's my job," the Gunny said. "Your job is to figure out the *what*. My job is to figure out the *how*."

McCoy chuckled. "Okay then, Gunny. Point made. How'd the count go?"

"We've got five total inside before we closed the door," the Gunny stated, ticking them off on one hand. "Kirby, Grimes, Frandsen – I found it ironic when we dropped on Alpha Centauri Prime and recalled that Frandsen's nickname was Bigfoot, didn't you? – myself, and you, sir."

"Kids," McCoy said and rubbed his face with an open palm. "A corporal, a freshly-minted sergeant and a private first class."

"Well, *I'm* not a kid, sir," the Gunny reminded him. "Haven't been for a very long time."

"Thank God, I'm not the only one with gray hair," McCoy chuckled softly.

"Indeed, sir. We've picked up something

interesting, but I'm not getting too excited about it just yet. Sensors suggest that there's one life-form down here with us, and it's human, thank God," the Gunny said as he led the lieutenant down a new tunnel. He patted the sensor strapped to his belt.

"That makes sense," McCoy nodded, thinking back to what he could remember of Lemura, one of the oldest city-states on Earth. "Whatever was left of the elite class in Lemura would've come here when things went south. They knew they'd be dead if they didn't."

"Sensors have been wrong in the past, sir," Gunny reminded him. "Shouldn't be too much further. Whoever is left down here is making it easy for us. They don't appear to be moving, just staying in the same spot. Almost like they're waiting on us to come to them, sir." McCoy and the Gunny continued walking until they reached a set of sealed blast doors at the corridor's end.

"Gunny Iffland, will you do the honors?" McCoy asked and motioned at the thick steel doors.

The Gunny struck the center of the doors with the butt of his rifle three times. The clang of reinforced ceramic on metal echoed in the confined space. "Open up! This is Gunnery Sergeant Jonny Iffland of the United World Defense Force! If this door is not open in ten seconds, I will be forced to use drastic measures!"

"Drastic measures, Gunny?" McCoy raised an eyebrow.

"Indeed, sir," the Gunny said in a somber tone. "I will be forced to raise my voice."

"And that would be bad..." McCoy nodded, though he was not quite certain where the Gunny was going with this. The two men took a step back away from the door.

"My raised voice involves a polymer-bonded explosive device, sir," the Gunny clarified. McCoy grinned.

"Ah, yes, that would definitely get the point across."

The small circular lock on the front of the two doors dilated open, and the massive steel barriers disappeared into the concrete walls to reveal an old man in the tattered remnants of what once had been an elaborate uniform. Long, greasy gray hair spilled over the man's shoulders and down his back. His fingernails were ragged and overgrown, his eyes wild, almost feral. His beard was straggly and unwashed. The old man's eyes bugged as he took in the sight of the two armed soldiers.

McCoy felt as if someone had punched him in the gut as the recognition of just who the man standing before them was.

"Holy crap," he blurted. "You're Minister of War. You're Andre Yeltsin!"

The man's responding cackle was loud and extremely disturbing. "It's been a long time since anyone has called me that. Hasn't it been? Oh yes, it has."

McCoy and the Gunny stared at Lemura's Minster of War as the old man rubbed the palms of his hands together. His eyes, which seemed mildly less mad than moments before, were jumping between the two men before him.

"I know you," Yeltsin said and jabbed a finger at McCoy. "I watched you. You're from the *Argo*, aren't you? I saw it drop into orbit not long ago. Months, years... days? No, hours. It's all so very quantumly-connected now, isn't it? Come, come, you must be tired. Let me get you something to drink." Yeltsin ushered them into what appeared to be makeshift quarters of some kind. "I go by Governor Yeltsin now, though truth be told, there's not much left to be governor of."

"Do you remember me, sir?" McCoy asked, his eyes watching the not-quite-sane man in front of him warily. "I served under you at the Battle of the Canal, down in Latin America?"

"McCoy, James. You were fresh out of boot, a young PFC, before your were mustanged up to officer in the aftermath due to your exceptional leadership skills." Yeltsin grinned. "I never forget a face." Yeltsin poured two glasses of a stout smelling whiskey and offered the drinks to them. Both men declined.

"A lot has changed since the *Argo* left Earth, as you may have noticed. Pacifica and Atlantica both fell. Lemura is just about gone. I don't know how many survivors are buried in the rubble, hiding, praying for some sort of miracle. A miracle which *I* can guarantee!" Yeltsin laughed. "The Kaiju only *think* they've won this war. They assume that humanity is finished, and that we no longer fight because we are defeated. But that is not how humans fight. We pull back, lick our wounds, and come up with newer, better ways to defeat our enemy. I still have an ace up my sleeve to be played, and I am so glad you gentlemen are here to see it."

"Uh, Governor Yeltsin, sir," McCoy said, looking over at the Gunny for help. The stout gunnery sergeant shrugged helplessly, so McCoy struggled to find the right words without directly calling the old man crazy. "I think you may be mistaken slightly. The Kaiju *have* won the war, sir. The *Argo* will be breaking orbit as soon as we're back onboard her."

Yeltsin shook his head, his face sad. "You really have no idea, do you? Entangled quantum mechanics dictates that this will end the threat once and for all. I've lived in the math, and I've seen the future."

"I'm afraid I don't understand what you mean, sir," McCoy replied. "The human race on Earth is finished, almost completely gone. This isn't our home, not anymore. It's time we left and found a new one. This planet belongs to the Kaiju now."

"We can still stop them, gentlemen," Yeltsin took one of the filled glasses of whiskey and downed it in one gulp. He grabbed the second. "There *is* time. It isn't quite strong enough to be free yet. Not yet. The time..."

McCoy sighed. He had assumed that anybody that he or the other soldiers could find might be a little off, but he had not anticipated running into Minister Yeltsin, or that he would be around the bend. "Sir, I really think it's time we were going. The *Argo* is waiting for us. We need to get back to the surface and call for an extraction so we can get home."

"Home?" the Gunny repeated the word before he started nodding. "You know, you're right, sir. The *Argo* is our home now, isn't it?"

Yeltsin's entire body stiffened suddenly, crushing the glass he held in his hand. Blood and whiskey dripped from where the broken shards cut into his flesh. "You fools!" he rasped, the wild look in his eyes back. "If it gets loose, not even the *Argo* will be safe! We have to activate the weapon before we leave. Don't you see? It has to be done at exactly the right moment as she's born or it will all have been nothing! They are already among us in the stars, but without her, they can't leave this system! Once she's born, they'll spread everywhere, across the galaxy and beyond. This universe will burn! There will not be a single planet for what's left of humanity to be safe!"

"Whoa... calm down, sir." McCoy advanced on Yeltsin slowly, his hands outstretched. He started wondering again if the former governor's prolonged isolation had driven him completely mad. McCoy was determined not to let the old man hurt himself more, but that could be a dicey proposition for him. In his day, Yeltsin had been one the best soldiers he'd ever seen in combat. If Yeltsin really wanted to hurt him, McCoy could only hope that the Gunny would be able to help restrain the governor. "Instead of yelling at us, why don't you try to explain what you're going on about? In not-quite-crazy words, sir."

Yeltsin's eyes were still wild, but he took a breath and looked down at his bloodied hand. He pulled an oily, filthy handkerchief from his pocket and wrapped it around his wounded hand. "The Earth..." his voice trailed off as he tried searching for the right words. "The Kaiju. They're linked, somehow. At first, I didn't understand it, or I refused to see it. Not sure, quite frankly. It's embarrassing. I should know this. I knew her, after all. I don't know if the Kaiju have always been a part of this planet from its creation, or if they're alien invaders who arrived later. What I do know though is that they're using it. The planet, I mean. While the *Argo* was away at Alpha Centauri, the war raged. The Mother Kaiju grew larger and more numerous. But you see, all of it, the Mother Kaiju, the Dog Kaiju, the war... none of it really mattered. There was a sort of Overmind controlling all of the monsters. Or at least, that was the theory. We thought we had destroyed it, maybe even won the war, but we hadn't. That Overmind creature was just a small piece of the *real* Kaiju, like all the others. She was incubating, for lack of a better term, near the planet's core along."

The Gunny's expression told McCoy that the older soldier clearly thought the former governor was mad. McCoy couldn't help but be pulled in by the old man's words, though. Even in the depths of the man's madness, something true and terrifying niggled at the edge of his soul.

"She's awake now, boys," Yeltsin continued. "Stirring and getting ready to... I don't know, be born? When she does, this planet will die. She'll spread her wings and take to the stars, moving on to the next world. She will leave this husk behind, lifeless, empty... dead."

"Just how big is... she?" McCoy asked, curious in spite of himself.

"Larger than the *Argo*, that's for damn sure,"

Yeltsin laughed. "She'll rip this world apart as she leaves it. At least, a very large section of it, and the damage to the atmosphere and outer core will be irreparable. If the *Argo* is in orbit when that time comes, and we don't use the weapon I've worked at finishing all these years, mankind will truly be wiped out from existence. It may not be today, or even tomorrow, but she will find us. And she will finish us, once and for all."

"You don't really believe all this, do you sir?" the Gunny asked McCoy. "If I may make a suggestion, sir? Let's just take him and go. We can listen to his stories later, but we need to get back to the *Argo*. We found what the signal was. Mission accomplished."

"You have to listen to me, McCoy," Yeltsin pleaded, tears forming in his eyes. "The weapon is our only hope at existing."

McCoy frowned but decided that he could spare a few more moments. "Just what is this weapon, sir?"

"It's a planet killer, son, and it'll destroy the Earth. And the mother of all the Kaiju with it."

*****

"Phoenix Two, this is Phoenix Three," Commander Brad Handley called out over his comm.

"Go Three," came the reply from his longtime wingman.

"Fritz... you getting what I'm getting here?" Handley asked as he banked the Phoenix into a wide turn. Below him lay the ruined city of Lemura. He checked his radar again, just to make sure he was not hallucinating or having a systems malfunction. The signatures were still there, and growing in strength and number.

"Yeah, I got it," Lieutenant Commander Fritz Ling replied in a hushed tone. "I thought my systems were out of whack."

"I think... I count twenty of them. Repeat, two-zero of..."

"I wish I could say that I think that you're wrong, Three. But I think you're right. Let's hope that the *Argo* is paying attention up there."

"I hope Lieutenant McCoy hurries up. I want to get out of here as fast as possible," Handley muttered. Twenty feet behind and ten down, his wingman silently agreed as more large, unidentified blips appeared on the radar screens. Handley switched frequencies and hailed the *Argo*. "*Argo*, this is Phoenix Three. Do you read?"

"I've got you, Three," *Argo* replied instantly. "Looks like twenty Mothers coming your way."

"Roger that, *Argo*. That's what we counted too," Handley said as he pulled the Phoenix into a steady climb. "Do we engage or leave them be?"

"We still have men inside Lemura, Three," the *Argo* reminded him. "Can you delay the Mothers?"

"Phoenix Flight, this is McCoy," a new voice cut through the radio chatter. Handley toggled his comm.

"This is Phoenix Three, Lieutenant. Go ahead."

"One survivor found, requesting evac at secondary LZ."

"Roger that. Be warned that there are Mother Kaiju in the area."

"Well, that's just super fun fantastic. How many do you have, Three?" McCoy asked.

"Enough to make me wish we had about fifty nukes," Handley replied as he leveled the Phoenix out, Fritz staying just behind him. "Be at the secondary LZ in fifteen minutes, McCoy. Three out."

Using the sun to make spotting them difficult, Handley peered down at the ground and then out at ocean surrounding Lemura. He could see the large Mothers slowly making their way towards the shores. A small cluster of three was much closer to Lemura than the others were, and would reach the city before McCoy and the survivors would reach the LZ. He flipped frequencies.

"Fritz, we gotta slow those Mothers down," Handley said. "I may have been a little too optimistic when I told McCoy fifteen minutes."

"Roger that," Fritz agreed. "But we're transports, not Tridents. It's one thing to hose some Dogs. It's an entirely different thing to drop a Mother."

"We've got Hellfire missiles," Handley said. "That might do something."

"They might. More than likely it'll just piss one of those Mothers off. You know, someone's going to look over our flight recorders one day and get on us about a lack radio discipline," Fritz laughed.

"Screw 'em," Handley growled. "They're not down here."

"All right, switching over to Hellfires," Fritz said.

"Let's begin our attack approach," Handley said as the two Phoenixes began to dive down towards the approaching Mother Kaiju. G-forces pushed him back into the pilot's seat as the large shuttle increased speed. He flipped on the guidance system of the Phoenix and listened as the system began to warble at him. Moments later, the warble turned into a growl, signaling that the Hellfire had acquired the target. "Lead target acquired. Fox One! Fox One!"

Two AGM-114K high explosive anti-tank missiles released from the stubby wings of the shuttle and darted forward, their engines accelerating the missiles to over the speed of sound in less than two seconds. The small computer chips in each missile head targeted the lead Mother, identifying the center mass as the best place to explode.

Each of the three Mother Kaiju was a different kind of walking nightmare. The tallest stood over three hundred feet and had a hulking mass that was nearly as wide. Its body was similar to that of a twisted version of a crab that walked on two legs. Its pincers snapped as the midday sunlight reflected off the thick, sleek edges of its exoskeleton. It led the small pack of Mothers towards Lemura.

To its left was a strange mix of a fish and a wingless bird. Two glassy eyes stared at the ruined city, ignoring the two approaching shuttlecraft. A beak, sharp and pointed, protruded from the Mother's face. Scales covered the body, and it moved very much like a chicken as it followed its much-larger kin.

The last of the three Kaiju was the strangest. It

had no legs that Handley could see. The Mother was a large, lumbering jellyfish. Hundreds of smaller tentacles writhed and flopped about in the air around it, growing from the transparent central mass that passed for its body. It had no discernible eyes or mouth.

The two Hellfire missiles struck the lead Mother square in the armored chest plates, the high-explosive warhead exploding on the surface of the thick armor. The explosion was so bright that Handley was forced to turn his head to avoid losing his vision to the light. The crab Kaiju staggered, its exoskeleton fractured where the missiles impacted. The thing let out a shriek of pain and anger that could be heard inside both of the Phoenixes miles away.

"Well, that got its attention," Handley muttered. "Six Hellfire missiles left. You loaded for bear, Fritz?"

"Roger that."

"Let's light 'em up," Handley said. "Fox One!"

Fourteen missiles launched near-simultaneously from the two shuttles. Eight seconds later, the missiles followed the same path that the initial volley had and exploded on the damaged chest plate of the massive crab Kaiju. The beast staggered and dropped to one knee, chunks of plate and meat falling to the ground from where it was injured. It still did not fall, however, and the two Phoenixes screamed past the trio and began to circle around to the other side of Lemura.

"Well, that sucked," Fritz complained over the comm. "I thought I'd at least kill one of them.

"I'm not that surprised, not really," Handley stated. "The Hellfire was obsolete before the fall of Nor-wic. And Mag cannons? Dogkiller suits carry those. Worthless on something our size. You'd think we'd have more updated weaponry on these pieces of–"

"Phoenix Flight, this is *Argo*. Those Mothers barely slowed down!"

"Kinda noticed, *Argo*. Hope you have something you can drop on them," Handley suggested.

"We have kinetics, Phoenix Flight, but they'll wipe out everything – including the men you're about to extract."

"Yeah, let's hold off on that for a moment, *Argo*. We're gonna do all we can, *Argo*. Three, clear." Handley killed the transmission.

"So now what do we do?" Fritz asked, as they circled back to get another look at the trio of Mothers who were now drawing dangerously close to the city.

"What do we do? We pray, and hope that McCoy and the rest of his team are at the extraction point when we get there."

*****

"I'm sorry, Kitty," Dr. Mera Babineaux said through the speaker. "The contagion is too widespread. There's nothing we can do. I can't even isolate any individual enzyme in it to know where to begin. This... *stuff* has nothing I've ever seen before or anybody else on the Medical Board. I'm truly sorry. Do you have any... religious preferences for your... you know."

"No."

"I'll keep looking, because we might come across something like this again," Dr. Babineaux said in a soft tone. "But... sweetie, there aren't even any protein compounds I recognize in this thing!"

"Thanks for doing your best, Doc," Kitty sighed. She turned and shuffled back to the small cot. She picked up her tablet and continued work on decoding the space station's codes and data information. After a few minutes of trying to stare at the dancing numbers and symbols on the screen, Kitty powered down the tablet in her lap. She couldn't work anymore. The data was just swimming around the tablet's screen before her eyes, her brain refused to process the information on the screen. Her skin was slick with a sticky sweat that matted her hair to her scalp.

Her bowels burned like the fires of a furnace, and yet nothing she ate or drank came out. Her joints ached and throbbed constantly, though it was the low-grade fever she had developed over the past two hours that scared her more. Kitty had watched several of the other members of the group that had returned from Tango Zeta 3 break due to the fever and began to undergo the change. Scales had replaced their flesh, the pupils of their eyes becoming swirling pools of endless darkness. Only one soldier had broken free of the decontamination unit's restraints so far. Kitty thanked whatever deity was watching over the *Argo* that the guards on duty had been ready for it. They had cut down the poor escapee mere feet from her shattered decontamination chamber. Their guns had done a number on her already twisted and rearranged body, severing one of the two large fins that replaced her arms.

Even in death, the malformed rows of razor-sharp teeth that lined her mouth snapped and chewed at the *Argo's* artificial atmosphere from some lingering twitch of the woman's mutated nervous system. It had terrified Kitty to watch that, to know that the transformation would be her ultimate fate.

Regret stung Kitty. She knew she would never finish decrypting the logs and sensor data from the station that Captain Whitmire so sorely needed. Sure, she knew that someone else on board the *Argo* might do it eventually. However, it had been *her* task, her responsibility, and it hurt her to know that she had failed. Her life was over. In less than an hour at the average progression rate, she too would become one of *those* things like Fletcher and all of the others who had set foot on that cursed space station. They had all died on Tango Zeta 3, and nobody had known it at the time.

Fletcher began to hammer a spiked fin against the Plexiglas of his decontamination unit, long strings of saliva hanging from the extra mouths that covered the bulk of his face. His tan skin had become a dead gray and his rage nearly uncontainable. Spider web cracks were beginning to form in the Plexiglas of his decontamination unit from his relentless attack on it. Soon, the doctors and guards would be forced to put him down before he broke free and endangered the rest of *Argo's* crew, as they had with all of the others.

So far, only Kitty was still in control of her higher functions and not being driven by the baser urges which seemed to compel the others. She just wished there was something she could do, something to help the *Argo* and the rest of the colonists and crew who were still in hibernation. She hated the helpless feeling, which threatened to overwhelm her.

"No."

Her own voice startled her. She hadn't realized she had spoken, or that she had stood up. She glanced at the tablet in her hands and wondered why she had picked it up. A command sequence had been started on the tablet, one she was intimately familiar with: a direct link to the ship's AI, Medea. She glanced over the command/control sequence and nodded. Not only what she was doing was right, it was necessary. It was for the greater good.

She activated every single fire suppression system in the isolation chambers, including hers. Medea tried to stop her, but Kitty easily forced the AI to accept her command. Thick, treated liquid began to fill all twenty decontamination units, causing the scientists and guards to step back in surprise. Shouting began as it became evident that no one knew what was going on. No one but Kitty, at least.

Once the liquid was at knee-level in every occupied cell, and every single contaminated soul was touching it, she knew it was time. She closed her eyes and wished that the *Argo* would make it to wherever humanity was destined to rebuild, and that all those who were sure to look into the matter after the fact would understand her actions.

She pushed the "execute" button and every single electrical conduit in the decontamination cells overloaded. The liquid, in contact with the conduits, turned into a conductor as electricity coursed throughout the cells – causing over one hundred thousand volts of electricity to pass directly through every single infected's nervous system, overloading their bodies and causing each and every one of them to fall into the liquid, dead before they landed.

*****

Deep beneath the Earth's mantle in the outer core, a great being stirred. It rolled over in the flowing ocean of magma that it embraced, consciousness finally returning. The core's heat was comforting, but it knew the time had come to leave and take to the stars once more. It had slumbered enough. The body of the creature began to spasm as it pushed through the outer core and into the Earth's mantle. It delayed there for a minute as the environment changed around it.

It would delay no longer. The ocean floor split and heaved upwards as she rose from her nesting place. The water was superheated and flash-boiled the instant the billions of tons of magma pushed through in the creature's wake. The ocean floor split and heaved upwards as it rose from the nesting place.

Magma turned into lava and the super-heated liquid rock poured into the black, frigid depths of the ocean. The lava began to explode as the magma interacted with the ice cold waters, triggering a chain reaction all across the length of the Marianas

Trench as thousands of detonations began to daisy-chain for over 2,500 kilometers. The kinetic energy from each explosion was equivalent to three megatons of TNT per explosion. The entire region began to shake and collapse as more magma filled the Pacific Basin, triggering more explosions.

Giant wings unfurled and pushed the creature through the water and into the sky. Underwater blasts began to trigger massive tsunamis, pushing water away from the source of the eruptions and causing massive underwater swells that had not been seen in thousands of years to rush across the broken seabed.

In the air above the turbulent oceans, water, lava and mucous dripping from the massive wings, the creature slowly turned to the east and began to fly. The world crumbled and burned in the Kaiju's wake. The sky turned to ash, the waters boiled, and on the bridge of the *Argo*, Captain Nathan Whitmire could only stand and watch helplessly.

The Mother of All had risen. Humanity's time on Earth had run out.

*****

McCoy raced after Yeltsin, cursing himself for allowing the old man to get away from him. His respect for Yeltsin had kept him from seeing just how mad the former Minister of War truly was. Sending the Gunny up closer to the surface to direct the extraction on the Phoenixes had allowed him time to talk one on one with the old man. McCoy thought he had managed to convince Yeltsin to come with them, but Yeltsin had merely played on his trust, admiration and respect. McCoy rubbed at his jaw while he ran. The old man sure could still throw a mean punch. He was lucky he wasn't unconscious on the floor.

Time was running out. The lieutenant needed to get Yeltsin, drag the old man, if necessary, to the bunker's main door, and haul him onboard one of the shuttles. Yeltsin was fast for his age, which surprised McCoy. Panting, McCoy rounded another corner in the mass of seemingly random hallways that composed the interior of the bunker and saw Yeltsin outside a new set of blast doors, ones that he had not seen before. The old man was fiddling with a set of key cards, trying to open them. He managed to activate the doors just as McCoy reached him. Plowing into Yeltsin like a runaway train, he slammed the old man into the corridor's wall, pinning him there. Yeltsin struggled against him, fighting back like a cornered, rabid animal.

"Look!" Yeltsin screamed. "Look in there! That weapon is humanity's only hope!"

"Son of a bitch," McCoy growled as he fought with Yeltsin. The Minister left him no other choice. McCoy head butted the old man. The front of McCoy's combat helmet smashed into Yeltsin's forehead. The old man's eyes rolled up to show only whites, before falling closed and the former Minister of War went limp in his arms. McCoy caught his collapsing form. He started to drag Yeltsin back the way they had came, but as he did, he noticed the strange light pouring from the doorway that Yeltsin had opened. Placing the old man's body gently on the floor, McCoy moved to look inside the room. In the center, a glowing orb of pure energy spun, hovering a good seven feet off the floor.

"Oh. Oh, holy crap," McCoy breathed. He had never seen anything like it before. Energy danced and crackled about the orb, sending miniature lightning bolts to strike at the room's ceiling and floor. Four guide rods were around it, which seemed to attract most of the lightning bolts being tossed throughout the room. There was a control console just inside the doorway.

McCoy's eyes widened as he realized just what he was staring at. It had to be the weapon that the old man had kept going on about. Seeing it with his own eyes, it was easy to believe that the orb could destroy a planet, if its energy was unleashed. He backed away from the room and returned to where Yeltsin lay. *Was the old man's crazy ranting real?* He wondered. He shook his head. Even if it were, it didn't matter. The *Argo* was waiting, and it was past time to get the Hell off this planet.

McCoy heaved Yeltsin's limp form over his shoulders and ran through the corridors to where the other rest of the soldiers were waiting for him. The Gunny appeared relieved when as he saw them approaching.

"Did you hurt him much?" the Gunny asked as he picked up the Minister's limp head.

"I don't know," McCoy admitted. "You tell me. Is he concussed? Did I do any permanent damage?"

"Damn it, Jim," the Gunny growled. "I'm a Gunnery Sergeant, not some doctor!"

All the soldiers stood ready at the door to the surface and the streets of Lemura beyond. Outside, every single one of them knew that the Kaiju would be waiting. They would only have one shot at getting through them and to the shuttles which hovered nearby. If they missed their window of opportunity, the Dog Kaiju would tear them to shreds and eat their twitching bodies as they died.

"We're ready, sir," Kirby said from the point position. The young man was sweating profusely, but his voice was filled with iron resolve.

"Let's do this then," McCoy ordered. "I got the old man."

"You heard the LT," the Gunny grunted. "Let's blow this popsicle stand."

The door blew outward from the charges Kirby

and Grimes had rigged on it, clearing out the mass of Dog Kaiju on its other side. Given some breathing room, thanks to the explosion, the troops rushed out of the bunker. McCoy's breath caught in his throat as he saw all of the Mother Kaiju that had been drawn to the city. There were over half a dozen of the giant monsters closing on the bunker. One of the Phoenix shuttles lay in the street, destroyed. Its hull was caved inward and smoke billowed from the remains, drifting skyward. There was no sign of the pilot of the craft.

The second shuttle, hovered a dozen meters away from the position, nearly street-level as it waited with opens doors. Thousands of rounds of ammunition tore into the nearest Mother Kaiju in a desperate bid to slow her down long enough to allow the soldiers to board. The roar of the Mag cannon's continuous fire left McCoy's ears ringing. The Gunny was screaming something at him as a shadow fell over them all. McCoy couldn't make out the Gunny's words, only could tell that the Gunny was... afraid. He shook his head to clear it. The Gunny was never afraid, McCoy thought as a giant foot came down upon them. Something heavy broke him, caused him an immense flash of pain and agony that was indescribable. Then there was only darkness.

*****

Captain!" Tiffanie cried from the sensor station, where she was still assisting Yamilé.

Nathan did not need her warning, though. He saw the gigantic creature from his own display on his command chair. It was as large as the island of Pacifica and filled the *Argo's* main view screen. The mighty wings were over a hundred miles long from one tip to the other, and the beast's body was massive and bloated. The creature's lips were parted to show rows of glistening teeth as it streaked upwards from the Earth, the massive wings fighting against gravity so that it could escape to the stars.

The sight of the thing was enough to drive a sane person mad. The crew on the bridge around him began to panic. Some tried to cover their heads and not look at the screen, while others struggled simply to breathe. Yamilé clawed at her eyes with her fingernails, screaming at the top of her lungs as her mind simply snapped. The bridge crew's cries of fear echoed off the *Argo's* walls. Nathan forced himself to hold it together, but it was difficult, almost too difficult for the man.

"All hands, man your battle stations," his raspy voice echoed throughout the ship. Every single man and woman not in cryo heard his voice and the desperation in it, and hurried to their assigned station. The bridge's lighting switched to the red glow of emergency lights as he plopped into his command chair. "Target that abomination with everything we've got!"

Missile ports slid open all along the *Argo's*

forward hull as her rail guns began to blaze away at their maximum rate of fire, the electromagnetic guns firing tow ton tungsten-core bars of steel at the Kaiju every second. The gunners had not waited on his order to open fire, though Nathan didn't blame them. The beast was on a direct course for the *Argo*, and it was closing fast.

"Once you have a solution, fire at will," he told the missile crews. Over two hundred missiles flew from their respective ports in a staggered wave as some crews responded to the threat faster than others did. Bright blue flames could be seen propelling the missiles across the narrow divide between the *Argo* and the massive Kaiju.

Nathan's eyes were locked onto the screen as the missiles began to close in on the Kaiju. Everything seemed to slow to a crawl as the missiles, tiny icons of blue on his screen, moved closer and closer to the giant red blob on the opposite side of his monitor. His eyes drifted up to look at the visual display of the winged monster.

"Contact in three, two, one..." Tiffanie counted down for the benefit of those still willing to fight.

Almost every single missile fired struck the Kaiju dead on. The darkness of space lit up in a cacophony of atomic fire. The bright nuclear explosions overwhelmed the crew and blinded the *Argo's* sensors briefly. A panel started smoking near Nathan's command chair, which elicited a cry from the crewmember manning the station. Power on the bridge flickered briefly, which was indiscernible to the crew but created a massive problem at one particular station.

"Sensors offline!" Tiffanie yelled. The forward view screen had gone blank as well.

"Get those sensors back online now!" Nathan shouted at her, his hands squeezing the arms of his chair in a white-knuckled grip. It took every ounce of his willpower to stay seated and not launch himself across the bridge to fix the problem himself.

The screen flickered back to life just in time to reveal a flash of the Kaiju's razor-sharp teeth before they sank into the *Argo's* hull. The massive strike from the beast shook the entire ship and jerked it sideways in space, which did a number on their speed and orbital pattern. The members of the bridge crew who were not strapped into their seats were thrown about like ragdolls, bouncing against their consoles and tossed violently into the bridge's walls. The bridge filled with the sound of snapping bones and crashing bodies. Everywhere around him, people were crying out in pain or calling for help. Stations overloaded from power surges through the *Argo's* central systems and blew apart like small flash bombs. Fires raged in the dim red lights of the bridge.

"We... we hurt the thing, sir!" Hiro shouted from his station, which by the grace of God was still intact. Nathan looked around, his head swimming. He saw Tiffanie lying on the floor several feet from her station, her neck twisted in an awkward and unnatural angle as blood dripped from the corner of her open mouth. Her dull, lifeless gaze seemed to blame him for what had happened to both her and the *Argo*. The captain felt sick to his stomach, but he knew that his responsibilities were to the entire ship, and not just his bridge crew.

This included the thousands of souls he had sworn to keep alive.

He jumped from his seat and raced for the helm. The *Argo's* pilot was dead, her headless body strapped into her seat at the station. The chair was soaked in blood. A piece of the bridge's ceiling had collapsed and shaved the poor woman's head cleanly from her shoulders. The *Argo* continued to shake as alarms blared like air raid sirens. The Kaiju had hold of the *Argo* and it was pummeling the sturdy hull with its fists between slashes of her giant claws along the topside.

"Clearly, we didn't hurt her enough!" Nathan shouted at Hiro as he spun the chair containing the helmsman's corpse out of his way. Their only hope was to get away from the beast before it tore them completely apart and finished off humanity. An unprogrammed jump was dangerous, but he had been left with no other option. He had to keep everyone alive, no matter the cost to him. Nathan's fingers flew over the controls of the helm as he manually brought the warp engines online.

"Captain, this jump is unadvisable," Medea chimed in from the computer terminal. He scowled as he continued trying random combinations of coordinates, hoping one would work.

"I don't have a choice, Medea! If we don't, then this Kaiju will open us up and that'll be all she wrote, sweetheart! Poof! Humanity is done! Game over!"

He finished typing in the coordinates and pressed the confirmation button. The lighting on the bridge, already dim, turned nearly completely off as the engines drew almost all the available power to them. The Laws of Physics broke as space bent and blurred around the huge ship and the even larger monster still clinging to it.

The great Kaiju writhed and shuddered in pain as the jump bubble formed around the *Argo*. It released the ship as one of its mighty hands was severed at its wrist by the growing bubble of distorted energy and time. One last, defiant strike to the ship's hull rocked the entire vessel from bow to stern. The main view screen shattered into a mass of flying shrapnel. Shards of it caught Nathan in his right shoulder as he tried to turn away from the explosion. He fell to the floor with glass protruding from the ghastly injury, his own blood mixing with his deceased helmswoman. The shaking from the Kaiju stopped suddenly as everything around them turned sideway. The *Argo* blinked out of existence, leaving the dying home world of humanity far behind – and the Mother of All with it.

*****

An entire day had passed since the *Argo* escaped from Earth, and damage reports continued to come in, though not in the flood that they had initially. The captain had been discharged from sickbay and returned to duty, much to the chagrin of the Medical Board. They wanted the captain to take more time off before going back to work. He ignored their advice, though, and found himself on the bridge a mere five minutes after being cleared for active duty once more.

Bandages were wrapped around his right shoulder and his arm was set against his chest in a sling. Still, he worked on. The *Argo's* engines were fried, the power surge that had given them their unplanned jump overloading the circuitry which drove them. It would take weeks, if not longer, and more than a little luck to get them online and fully functional again. That, he recalled, was the *good* news.

Thousands of colonists and crew had perished in cryo-sleep. The great Kaiju had gotten lucky during her attack, and had crushed and mauled one entire section of the ship. That second just happened to contain almost a third of the colonists who had originally been meant for Alpha Centauri Prime.

Over half the active crew was either dead or injured as well, but they followed the lead of their captain and continued to work through the pain and suffering that they all were dealing with.

He stood, staring out into the vastness of space on the repaired view screen before him. He knew that mankind's destiny lay in the stars, had known this since he was a child. However, the Mother of All, as he had taken to thinking of her, had planted a tiny seed of doubt in his heart. He did not know where she would go, or what she would do. He knew that the *Argo* had hurt her badly. Would she find another planet to take over, or would she try to follow the *Argo* through space and time? He didn't know. Nobody had ever been able to read the alien mind of a Kaiju. The best anyone could do was guess.

6,107 men, women and children.

That was all that was left of humanity. It was his job to find them a new home, and to keep them alive. It was a dangerously low number, one that concerned the scientists who were already creating breeding programs, much to his chagrin. He had thought that, as a species, humanity was above such things. He had never considered the potential disruptions that could arise if women were forced to bear children, or that computer models would have to be drafted in order to prevent any sort of inbreeding. He had been sure humanity would survive, once. Now? He was no longer sure of anything.

They were alive, for now. For how much longer, Nathan thought, was anybody's guess.

"And all day long and all night, the wind bore the ship on, blowing fresh and strong," Whitmire whispered as he stared into the dark abyss of space. He fiddled with the bandages of his shoulder with his mobile hand. "But when dawn rose, there was not even a breath of air. And they marked a beach jutting forth from a bend of the coast, very broad to behold, and by dint of rowing came to land at sunrise."

Much like the *Argo* of old, only sheer determination would take them home.

Wherever that ended up being.

The End